BATTLING COVID-19

A New NORMAL

Life after COVID-19

RACHAEL L. THOMAS

Checkerboard
Library

An Imprint of Abdo Publishing
abdobooks.com

abdobooks.com

Printed in the United States of America, North Mankato, Minnesota
102020
012021

THIS BOOK CONTAINS
RECYCLED MATERIALS

Design: Sarah DeYoung, Mighty Media, Inc.
Production: Mighty Media, Inc.
Editor: Jessica Rusick
Cover Photograph: Shutterstock Images
Interior Photographs: Alain Pitton/AP Images, p. 17; Capt. Cassandra Mullins/The National Guard/Flickr, p. 25; Dan Keck/Flickr, p. 6 (bottom); Elvert Barnes/Flickr, p. 7; Geber86/iStockphoto, p. 23; John Rucosky/AP Images, p. 13; Science Source, p. 27; Shutterstock Images, pp. 5, 6, 9, 18, 19, 21; Ted Soqui/AP Images, pp. 7 (top), 15; Tom Witham/USDA/Flickr, p. 11; Virginia Mayo/AP Images, p. 29
Design Elements: Shutterstock Images

Library of Congress Control Number: 2020940242

Publisher's Cataloging-in-Publication Data
Names: Thomas, Rachael L., author.
Title: A new normal: life after COVID-19 / by Rachael L. Thomas
Other title: life after COVID-19
Description: Minneapolis, Minnesota : Abdo Publishing, 2021 | Series: Battling COVID-19 | Includes online resources and index
Identifiers: ISBN 9781532194320 (lib. bdg.) | ISBN 9781098213688 (ebook)
Subjects: LCSH: COVID-19 (Disease)--Juvenile literature. | Social distance--Juvenile literature. | Interpersonal relations--Juvenile literature. | Social media--Juvenile literature. | Videoconferencing--Juvenile literature.
Classification: DDC 302.231--dc23

Contents

A Deadly Pandemic

On December 16, 2019, a woman in Wuhan, China, was hospitalized with a lung **infection.** Over the following weeks, hospitals in Wuhan reported more cases of the same illness. At first, doctors didn't know what was causing it.

Scientists soon discovered that a new coronavirus was spreading through Wuhan. This virus caused a disease called COVID-19. In the following months, COVID-19 spread to other countries. It soon infected millions of people around the world. On March 11, 2020, the **World Health Organization (WHO)** declared COVID-19 a **pandemic**.

COVID-19 changed the lives of people in the United States and around the world. Experts **predicted** that some aspects of everyday life would return to normal after the pandemic. But other aspects would never be the same. The world would have to adapt to a new normal.

WHAT IS A CORONAVIRUS?

Coronaviruses are a large group of viruses that cause **respiratory** illnesses. Most coronaviruses exist only in animals. However, several have spread from animals to humans. The coronavirus discovered in Wuhan is called severe acute respiratory syndrome coronavirus 2 (SARS-CoV-2). It causes a disease called coronavirus disease 2019, or COVID-19. COVID-19 spreads when saliva droplets pass from person to person. This can happen when someone coughs, sneezes, sings, breathes, or talks. Most people with COVID-19 do not suffer serious **symptoms**. But some people develop life-threatening problems. Because of this, the virus is viewed as a threat to world health.

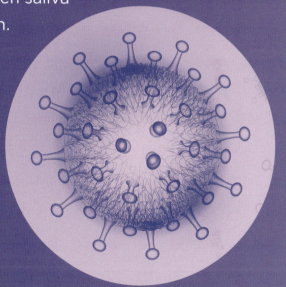

TIMELINE

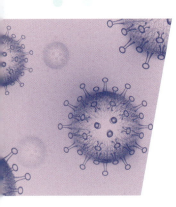

DECEMBER 16, 2019

One of the earliest known COVID-19 patients is admitted to a hospital in the city of Wuhan, China.

MARCH 30, 2020

More than half of all US states are under stay-at-home orders.

MARCH 12, 2020

Major League Baseball cancels its spring games.

JANUARY 31, 2020

The US government bans travel from China to the United States.

MARCH 12, 2020

Ohio governor Mike DeWine orders all schools in the state to close. He is the first US governor to do so.

MARCH 11, 2020

The World Health Organization (WHO) declares COVID-19 a pandemic.

EARLY APRIL 2020

Global carbon dioxide (CO_2) emissions are 17 percent lower than they were in April 2019. This is due to a decrease in vehicle and factory emissions during the pandemic.

EARLY JUNE 2020

Most US states have lifted their stay-at-home orders.

APRIL 3, 2020

The Centers for Disease Control and Prevention (CDC) recommends that people wear face masks in public.

LATE APRIL 2020

Pakistan approves the Green Stimulus Plan. It creates jobs for people in Pakistan who are unemployed because of the pandemic.

OCTOBER 2020

More than 1 million people around the world have died from COVID-19.

The World Changes

World leaders made efforts to slow the spread of COVID-19 in early 2020. Travel was one of the first activities affected by the COVID-19 **pandemic**. On January 31, the US government banned travel from China to the United States. As COVID-19 spread, more countries closed their borders to foreign travelers.

Soon, people with travel plans weren't the only ones affected. In March, the **Centers for Disease Control and Prevention (CDC)** recommended that Americans practice social distancing. This meant staying at least six feet (2 m) away from other people in public. It also meant avoiding large gatherings. On April 3, the CDC also recommended that people wear face masks in public. These precautions would help slow the spread of COVID-19.

STEM CONNECTION

The CDC recommended that anyone sick with COVID-19 stay home. However, people could spread COVID-19 without ever showing **symptoms** of the disease. Face masks prevented people from accidentally spreading COVID-19 to others. Masks help contain droplets from a person's nose and mouth. These droplets can spread COVID-19.

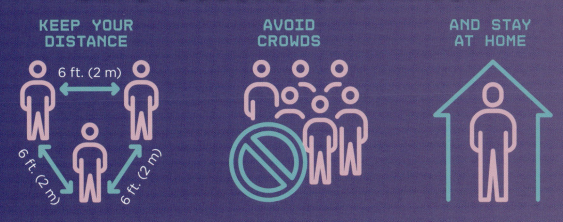

HOW TO PRACTICE
SAFE SOCIAL DISTANCING

KEEP YOUR DISTANCE

6 ft. (2 m)

6 ft. (2 m)

6 ft. (2 m)

AVOID CROWDS

AND STAY AT HOME

Many large events were canceled to enforce social distancing. On March 12, Major League Baseball canceled its spring games. Singers such as Taylor Swift and Justin Bieber delayed their concerts until 2021. Large festivals and parades were also canceled across the country.

Also on March 12, governor Mike DeWine ordered schools in Ohio to close. Schools in other states soon closed as well. So, many students began attending school online. By March 30, most US state governors had issued stay-at-home orders. Citizens were asked only to leave their homes for **essential** travel.

Nonessential businesses also closed under stay-at-home orders. These included hair salons and movie theaters. Closing nonessential businesses limited COVID-19's spread in public spaces. Essential businesses were allowed to remain open. These included grocery stores, healthcare facilities, and factories. Companies with offices remained open only if their employees could work from home. That way, COVID-19 would not spread in office spaces.

These **restrictions** helped slow the spread of COVID-19. But they also meant people had to adjust to new routines. This adjustment was difficult for many. People could not visit friends and family. Some students had trouble focusing on online lessons. And, many parents had to work at home while caring for young children.

Another challenge was Americans' different reactions to **pandemic** guidelines. Some people tried to accept the new normal. However, others were upset about face mask rules and stay-at-home orders. This sometimes led to arguments in personal, public, and professional settings.

Many people wanted life to return to normal. But normal seemed a long way away. So, Americans had to adapt to life at home. There were many challenges. But there were also benefits.

Almost 30 million US children participate in the National School Lunch Program. During the pandemic, many schools continued to provide free meals to students who needed them.

COVID-19 and Community

COVID-19 caused many challenges. But the **pandemic** had positive effects too. People traveled less frequently under stay-at-home orders. As a result, many reported feeling more connected to their local communities.

People also came together to support high-risk community members. High-risk people were more likely to develop a serious case of COVID-19. These groups included people over 65 years old. Those with certain health conditions were also at risk. These conditions included kidney disease and high blood pressure.

Communities worked to keep these groups safe by performing tasks that would allow at-risk people to stay at home. One task was delivering groceries to elderly neighbors. Another was taking high-risk neighbors' pets to vet appointments. As a result, some people developed new friendships with their neighbors.

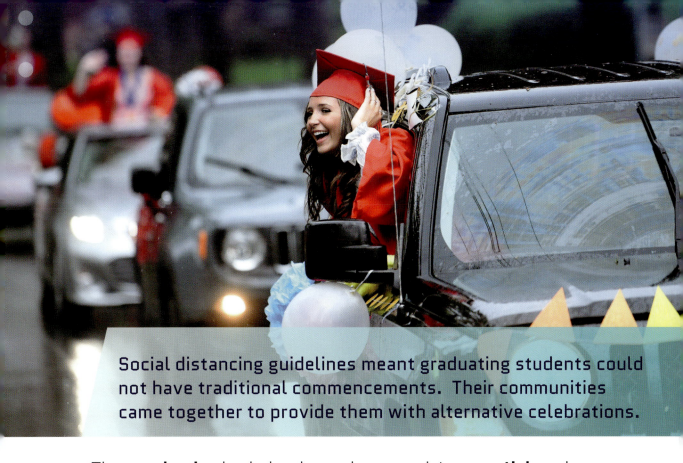

Social distancing guidelines meant graduating students could not have traditional commencements. Their communities came together to provide them with alternative celebrations.

The **pandemic** also helped people appreciate **essential** workers. These workers included delivery drivers, healthcare workers, and grocery store employees. Essential workers risked their lives to keep important services running. Many employers temporarily increased wages for essential workers. People also placed signs in their yards thanking essential workers.

A Green Future

The COVID-19 **pandemic** united communities. Some experts also believed it had a positive effect on the **environment**. By April, many countries had been forced into **lockdown**. Travel was **restricted**. This meant fewer vehicles were running. As businesses closed, fewer factories were operating. These effects of the pandemic led to reduced carbon dioxide (CO_2) emissions.

Vehicles and factories release large amounts of CO_2 into the atmosphere. CO_2 traps heat from the sun. This keeps the earth warm. However, most scientists say CO_2 emissions are too high. This causes Earth's temperature to increase.

Global warming has damaging effects on the environment. One effect is more animal extinctions. Another is more extreme weather events. Scientists say that reducing CO_2 emissions can help prevent global warming.

Because of the pandemic, global CO_2 emissions in early April were 17 percent lower than they had been in April 2019. Experts expected CO_2 emissions to increase again as lockdowns eased.

The skies over Los Angeles, California, were clearer than usual as fewer vehicles and factories operated.

However, many still saw the COVID-19 **crisis** as an opportunity to build a greener economy.

Countries across the world responded to this idea. Pakistan was one. In late April, Pakistani leaders approved the Green **Stimulus** Plan. The plan would create tree-planting jobs for people in the country left unemployed by COVID-19. Trees absorb CO_2. So, planting trees can help reduce the amount of CO_2 in the atmosphere.

On September 30, world leaders met virtually to discuss **biodiversity** loss. Around the world, humans were destroying natural habitats. Many plants and animals faced extinction. This biodiversity loss was bad for human health. Fewer plants and animals meant fewer food sources and medicines. Leaders said protecting nature should be a key part of COVID-19 economic recovery. They called on businesses and governments to protect biodiversity while rebuilding from the **pandemic**.

STEM CONNECTION

The average car emits about five tons (4.5 t) of CO_2 each year. A mature tree can absorb 50 pounds (23 kg) of CO_2 in one year. So, it would take around half an acre (0.2 ha) of forest to absorb the carbon emissions of one car!

In June 2020, people in France protested outside a factory to raise awareness about CO_2 emissions.

Global Impact

AUSTRIA

Austrians found ways to help students learn at home during the **pandemic**. In March, an Austrian television station began showing daily educational programs for students. A program for younger students aired in the morning. A program for older students aired in the afternoon.

ITALY

Italy's nationwide **lockdown** began on March 10. Most businesses closed. And, people were asked to stay home. People couldn't gather like normal. However, they still found ways to have fun. Across Italy, musicians played concerts from their windows. Neighbors also danced and sang together from their balconies.

SOUTH KOREA

In late May, many schools in South Korea reopened after being closed for months. The schools had safety measures in place to slow the spread of COVID-19. Students and teachers wore face masks. And, there were plastic dividers between desks.

INDIA

In 2019, India had the worst air pollution in the world. Car exhaust and smoke from factories made the air hazy. During the **pandemic**, many factories closed. And, fewer cars were on the road. So, air pollution decreased. The skies became clear. Citizens could even see the Himalayan mountain range from up to 100 miles (161 km) away.

Not Yet Normal

By mid-May, new COVID-19 cases were decreasing in many US states. Most states had lifted their stay-at-home orders by early June. This meant **nonessential** businesses could reopen. However, most had safety measures in place. For example, many stores required customers to wear face masks.

Despite safety measures, **infections** increased again during the summer. Throughout July, the US had record numbers of new daily cases. Cases continued to rise and decline throughout the fall. The **pandemic** was far from over.

Most experts said the pandemic would not end until scientists developed a COVID-19 vaccine. A vaccine would prevent people from getting the disease. By October, hundreds of vaccines were being tested. But none had been approved for wide use.

Scientists said a vaccine could be available early 2021. Until then, experts said COVID-19 **outbreaks** would continue. These would likely lead to more **lockdowns** and stay-at-home orders.

Experts believed these **restrictions** would have lasting effects on human behavior. The **pandemic** changed how people interacted. For example, people bumped elbows instead of shaking hands. This was to avoid spreading germs. Strangers also avoided one another on sidewalks to stay six feet (2 m) apart. Behavior experts believed these new habits would continue after the pandemic. Experts **predicted** that COVID-19 would cause other lasting changes as well.

HOW TO WEAR A FACE MASK

1. Wash your hands before putting the mask on.

2. Loop the mask's straps around your ears or over your head.

3. Adjust the mask to cover your mouth and nose. Make sure there are no gaps between your face and the mask.

The World Moves Online

During the COVID-19 **pandemic,** many people relied on the internet to do everyday business. People shopped online and had products delivered to their homes. They used video communication software to have doctor appointments from home. And, people used video-conferencing platforms such as Zoom to hold work meetings and attend school.

Before the pandemic, these online services were already becoming more popular. During the pandemic, their popularity exploded. In December 2019, Zoom had 10 million daily meeting participants. By March 2020, the platform had 200 million daily meeting participants.

Many experts **predicted** that increased online activity was part of a new normal. They believed that after the pandemic, people would continue to shop, work, attend school, and get medical help online more than ever before.

Online doctor appointments let people see a doctor without the risk of spreading or catching COVID-19.

Some experts worried that this new normal would worsen **inequality**. In April 2020, nearly 21 million Americans had no high-speed internet connection. Many were from low-income households. These people couldn't easily access online services. Some US lawmakers pushed for policy changes to help increase internet access across the country.

Voting by Mail

The COVID-19 **pandemic** also had the potential to change how Americans vote. The pandemic happened during a US presidential election year. Beginning in early 2020, people were voting in **primary** elections. These elections decided the candidates in the November presidential election.

The pandemic made voting in primary elections difficult. Usually, voters went to polling stations to vote. Polling stations were in public buildings. These included schools and churches. Thousands of voters entered these buildings during an election day. People often stood close together as they waited to vote.

Officials knew it would be hard to practice social distancing at polling places. So, some states encouraged people to vote through **absentee ballots**. Voters submit these ballots by mail. This way, people could vote from home.

During the 2016 US presidential election, nearly a quarter of the ballots cast had been mailed in. In 2020, experts expected more than half of all ballots to be mailed in. In fact, some **predicted**

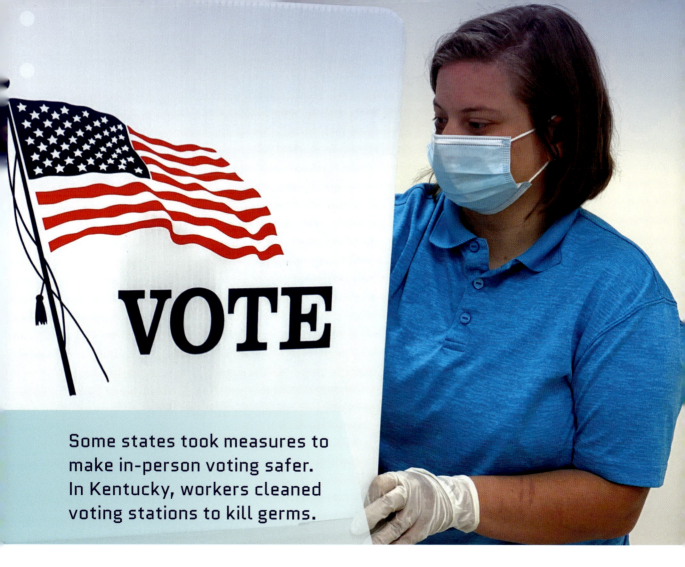

Some states took measures to make in-person voting safer. In Kentucky, workers cleaned voting stations to kill germs.

the 2020 election would change voting in future elections. One survey found that most Americans supported conducting all future elections by mail.

Planning for Pandemics

People adapted to life during the COVID-19 **pandemic.**
However, the world had not been ready for such a **crisis**. Many experts claimed world leaders should have been better prepared. For years, scientists had warned that a global pandemic could occur. Experts said nations needed better ways to detect new disease **outbreaks**.

One solution was the Global Virome Project (GVP). This program would study viruses found in wild animals, such as SARS-CoV-2. Researchers would add their findings on new viruses to a database. If a virus spread to humans, scientists could find information about it in the GVP's database. This would allow scientists to more quickly begin developing a vaccine.

Leaders also considered how to help businesses during future pandemics. Many businesses had temporarily closed under stay-at-home orders. Some businesses lost too much money.

A scientist in Nigeria collects bats to study new viruses.

They were forced to close permanently. These closures led leaders to discuss the need for **pandemic insurance**. This insurance would help businesses survive the economic impacts of future pandemics.

The New Normal

By October 2020, tens of millions of people around the world had been **infected** with COVID-19. More than 1 million had died. Countless others were affected by **lockdowns** and stay-at-home orders.

In the fall, some US schools opened for in-person learning. Students had to wear masks while attending school in person. Other schools continued with distance learning. And, many schools had a mix of at-home and in-school learning.

Meanwhile, scientists hoped to develop a COVID-19 vaccine that would end the **pandemic**. Once the pandemic was over, some aspects of life could return to normal. However, many people might continue to work, shop, and attend school and appointments from home.

It may be years before the effects of the COVID-19 pandemic are understood. But many people believe the global population can build a better world from the **crisis**. In the future, people may work harder to protect the **environment**. More homes may have access to online resources. And, the world may be better prepared for future challenges.

A scientist researches the SARS-CoV-2 virus to develop a vaccine.

Glossary

absentee ballot—a ballot submitted in advance by a voter unable to attend election day. A ballot is a piece of paper used to cast a secret vote.

biodiversity—the existence of many different plants and animals.

Centers for Disease Control and Prevention (CDC)—the main national health organization in the United States. The CDC works to control the spread of disease and maintain and improve public health in the United States and other countries.

crisis—a difficult or dangerous situation that needs serious attention.

environment—nature and everything in it, such as the land, sea, and air.

essential—very important or necessary. Something that is not essential is nonessential.

inequality—the quality of being unequal.

infection—an unhealthy condition caused by something harmful, such as a virus. If something has an infection, it is infected.

insurance—a contract that helps people pay their bills if they are sick, hurt, or affected by disaster. People with insurance pay money, usually monthly, to keep the contract.

lockdown—a temporary measure ordered by government officials in which people are required to stay at home and limit public contact.

outbreak—a sudden increase in the occurrence of an illness.

pandemic—worldwide spread of a disease that can affect most people.

predict—to guess something ahead of time on the basis of observation, experience, or reasoning.

primary—a method of selecting candidates to run for public office. A political party holds an election among its own members. They select the party members who will represent it in the coming general election.

respiratory—having to do with the system of organs involved with breathing.

restrict—to keep within certain limits. Something that does this is a restriction.

stimulus—something that encourages growth or activity.

symptom—a noticeable change in the normal working of the body. A symptom indicates or accompanies disease, sickness, or another malfunction.

World Health Organization (WHO)—an agency of the United Nations that works to maintain and improve the health of people around the world.

Online Resources

Booklinks
NONFICTION NETWORK
FREE! ONLINE NONFICTION RESOURCES

To learn more about the COVID-19 pandemic, please visit **abdobooklinks.com** or scan this QR code. These links are routinely monitored and updated to provide the most current information available.

Index